# Tom

## Written and illustrated by
# Tomie dePaola

SCHOLASTIC INC.

New York Toronto London Auckland Sydney

*For my sisters, Maureen Modine and Judie Bobbi,*
*and my cousins, Mary Downey Malavase and Sheila Woods.*

ISBN 0-590-48093-6

Copyright © 1993 by Tomie dePaola.
All rights reserved. Published by Scholastic Inc.,
555 Broadway, New York, NY 10012,
by arrangement with G.P. Putnam's Sons,
a division of The Putnam & Grosset Group.

12 11 10 9 8 7 6 5 4 3        4 5 6 7 8 9/9

Printed in the U.S.A.        09

First Scholastic printing, February 1994

Tommy's grandfather always used to say, "We're named after each other, Tommy. That's why I want you to call me Tom instead of Grandpa."

So Tommy did.

Tommy and his family went to visit Tom and Nana almost every Sunday. (Nana was Tommy's grandmother.)

And every Sunday for as long as Tommy could remember, Tom read the Sunday comics out loud. Tom used different voices, which made Tommy laugh and laugh. Sometimes Tom acted out funny poems. Tommy's favorite was "The Animal Fair."

"I went to the Animal Fair.
The Birds and the Beasts were there.
The big baboon by the light of the moon
would comb out his golden hair."

Tom would pretend to comb and comb long, long hair.
(He was bald.)

Tommy would get the giggles and as Tom went on, he giggled louder and louder. Sometimes he would squeal and laugh so loud that Tom would start laughing too.

"Tom Downey," Nana would say, "you're just as bad as that child."

Sometimes, if they were really loud, Nana would say, "Tom Downey, you're just as bad as that child, and the Downeys, and the rest of the Irish!"

When that happened, and it was winter, Tom would say, "C'mon, Tommy, let's go to the cellar and shake and sift the ashes." Tom and Nana had a big coal furnace, and Tom would shake the ashes to keep the coal burning. "Now we'll sift the ashes to get rid of the clinkers, and we'll save the ashes to put on the sidewalk if it gets icy."

Then Tom and Tommy would sit down near the warm furnace. Tom would light his corncob pipe (Nana wouldn't let him smoke it upstairs) and he would begin telling stories—some about himself when he was a little boy and some that he made up. (Tommy loved those the best.)

If it was not winter, they would just sit outside the cellar door and talk.

Once they went next door to the Lubys' and saw their puppies. "Those are firehouse dogs," Tom told Tommy. "Your great-uncle Jim had one when he was the fire chief. His name was Sparky and when the siren went off, he would run alongside the fire engine all the way to the fire."

Tom and Nana had a grocery store. Nana was in charge of the front of the store. Tommy helped put the cans of food on the shelves just the way Nana wanted them. "Nice and neat with the labels facing out."

Tom was in charge of the back of the store. He was a butcher and behind the counter was Tom's "butcher's table" where he cut up the meat for his customers.

Next to that was the big grinding machine. Tom would grind up pieces of beef into hamburger. Tommy liked to help him.

"Be careful now," Tom always said. "I don't want any fingers in my hamburger."

Sometimes when Tommy was there, Mrs. Novak brought in the chickens that his grandfather would sell. Their feathers were all plucked, but their heads and feet were still on. Tom would take his cleaver and WHOP—off came a head. WHOP—WHOP—off came the feet.

Once Tom gave Tommy a chicken head to take home. "See this?" he told Tommy. "Well, if you plant it in the garden and don't disturb it for three weeks, you'll have a chicken bush." Tom put it in a bag and tied it with string.

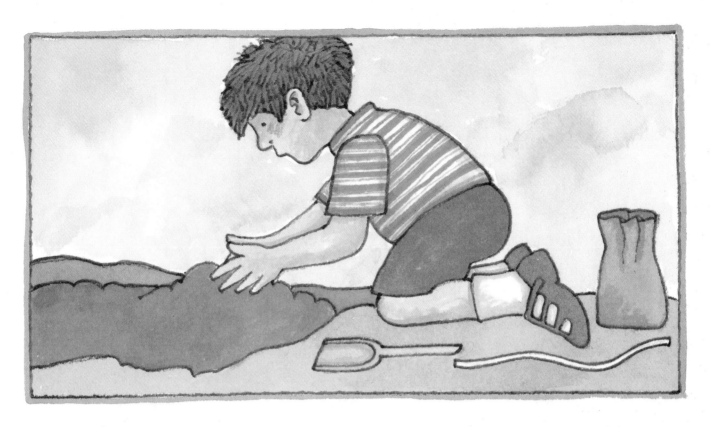

Tommy couldn't wait to get home and bury it. But, after only three days, he dug it up to see if anything was happening.

The next weekend, when Tommy told Tom that nothing was growing, Tom said, "Too bad. It will only work once." (He knew that Tommy couldn't wait three weeks without looking.) "But let me show you something else." He picked up a chicken foot.

"See that little white string thing? It's called a tendon. If you pull it, the chicken foot opens and closes. Try it." Tommy tried. It was scary, but it made him giggle. Tom put two chicken feet in a bag and tied it with string.

When Tommy got home, he washed the chicken feet with soap and a scrub brush. (They were kind of smelly.)

Then he asked his mother if he could borrow some of her nail polish.

"What for?" his mom asked.

"It's a secret," Tommy told her.

"All right, but don't spill it."

Tommy picked the brightest red and painted the claws on the chicken feet.

All weekend, Tommy practiced holding a foot in each hand and pulling the tendons. The chicken feet opened and closed. "Garunge–arunge–a…"

On Monday morning, Tommy hid the chicken feet in his pocket and went to school.

His best friend, Jeannie, was standing in the school yard. Tommy held a chicken foot in each hand and pulled his hands up in his sleeves so only the chicken feet stuck out. He put his arms in back of him.

"Hi, Jeannie," Tommy said.
"Hi," Jeannie answered.

"Garunge-arunge-a!"
"EEEK!" Jeannie screamed.

Three girls turned around to look.

"Garunge-arunge-a!" went Tommy and the chicken feet.

"EEEK! EEEK! EEEK!" the girls screamed.

Tommy turned.
"Garunge-arunge-a!"

"SCREECH!" It was a teacher.

Tommy spent the whole morning in the principal's office. She threw away his chicken feet and sent him home with a note:

The next weekend when Tommy went to visit Tom and Nana, Tommy told Tom all about it.

"Well," Tom said, "we'll just have to think of something else to do, don't you think?"

And Tom gave Tommy a big wink.